13.95

Crinkleroot's
BOOK OF
ANIMAL TRACKING

CRINKLEROOT

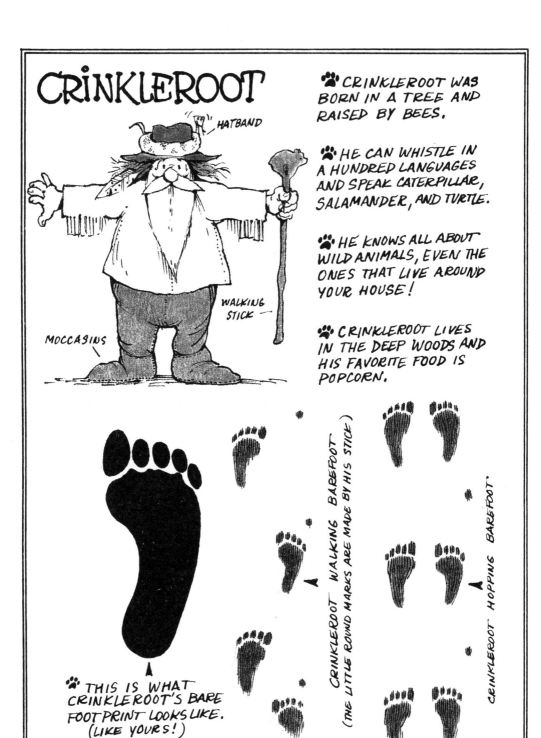

HATBAND

WALKING STICK

MOCCASINS

🐾 CRINKLEROOT WAS BORN IN A TREE AND RAISED BY BEES.

🐾 HE CAN WHISTLE IN A HUNDRED LANGUAGES AND SPEAK CATERPILLAR, SALAMANDER, AND TURTLE.

🐾 HE KNOWS ALL ABOUT WILD ANIMALS, EVEN THE ONES THAT LIVE AROUND YOUR HOUSE!

🐾 CRINKLEROOT LIVES IN THE DEEP WOODS AND HIS FAVORITE FOOD IS POPCORN.

🐾 THIS IS WHAT CRINKLEROOT'S BARE FOOT PRINT LOOKS LIKE. (LIKE YOURS!)

CRINKLEROOT WALKING BAREFOOT (THE LITTLE ROUND MARKS ARE MADE BY HIS STICK)

CRINKLEROOT HOPPING BAREFOOT

Crinkleroot's
BOOK OF
ANIMAL TRACKING

JIM ARNOSKY

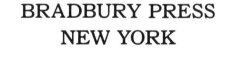

BRADBURY PRESS
NEW YORK

FOR MY FATHER AND MOTHER

Bradbury Press
An Affiliate of Macmillan, Inc.
866 Third Avenue, New York, NY 10022
Collier Macmillan Canada, Inc.
Crinkleroot's Book of Animal Tracking was originally published in 1979 by G. P. Putnam's Sons, in a 7 x 8 ¹/₂-inch format with black-and-white and two-color illustrations throughout, under the title *Crinkleroot's Book of Animal Tracks and Wildlife Signs.*
Printed and bound in Singapore
10 9 8 7 6 5 4 3 2 1

LIBRARY OF CONGRESS CATALOGING-IN-PUBLICATION DATA
Arnosky, Jim.
Crinkleroot's book of animal tracking/Jim Arnosky.
    p.cm.
    Rev. ed. of: Crinkleroot's book of animal tracks and wildlife
signs. c1979.
    Summary: Explains how to find and understand the signs made by animals around water, in the woods, and in the snow.
    ISBN 0–02–705851–4
    1. Animal tracks–Juvenile literature.   2. Tracking and trailing— Juvenile literature.   [1. Animal tracks.]   I. Arnosky, Jim.
Crinkleroot's book of animal tracks and wildlife signs.   II. Title.
QL768.A75   1989   599–dc19   88–15353   CIP   AC

CRINKLEROOT'S ANIMAL CHARTS

*H*ello. You've been following Crinkleroot tracks.
My name is Crinkleroot, and these are my tracks.

I can hear a fox turn in the forest, and spot a mole
hole on a mountain. I can find an owl in the daytime.

When I walk about the forest, I leave signs that tell I've been around—my footprints. Animals leave marks and tracks that show where they have been and what they have been doing.

I can show you how I find signs of animals that live near me; then you can find signs of animals that live near you. One of the best places to look is around water.

Animals are attracted to streams and ponds, park fountains, and even damp patches of grass. There they find water to drink and food to eat.

This pond was created by beavers. Can you see the beaver signs?

Beavers have sharp teeth and can gnaw down
a tree! Chewed-down trees and gnawed-off twigs
are good beaver signs to look for.

Beavers create a pond by damming up a stream,
using branches, sticks, and mud. A dam like this is a
sure sign that beavers are living in the pond.

When a beaver fells a tree that is too heavy to drag to the water, it chews the tree into small logs and rolls each one into the pond. The beaver then pushes the floating log to wherever it is needed. Sometimes a beaver gets lucky, and the tree falls right into the pond.

Beavers use logs and chewed-off branches to build their homes, or lodges.

Beavers also eat the wood from the trees they gnaw down. In autumn they gnaw off the small branches and store them on the bottom of the pond. In winter when the pond is frozen over, they will use these branches for food.

Let's wade around the shallow edges of the pond and look for other wildlife signs.

BEAVER

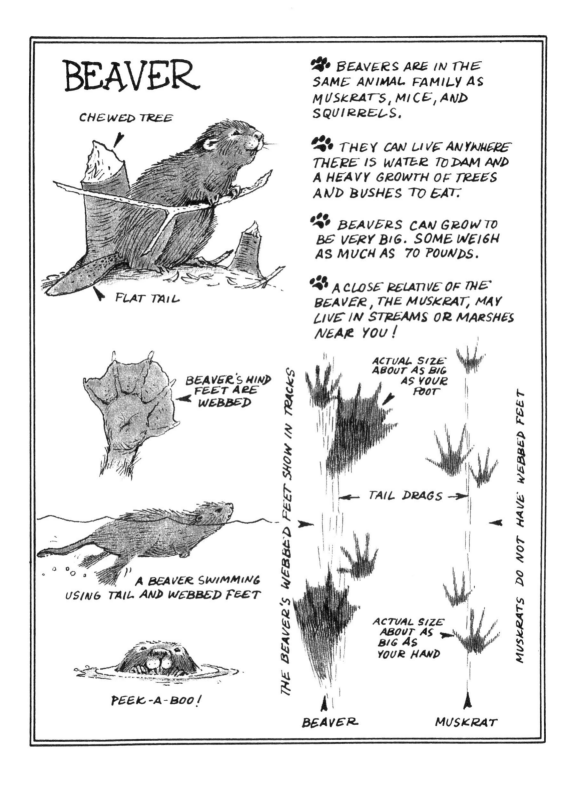

CHEWED TREE

FLAT TAIL

🐾 BEAVERS ARE IN THE SAME ANIMAL FAMILY AS MUSKRATS, MICE, AND SQUIRRELS.

🐾 THEY CAN LIVE ANYWHERE THERE IS WATER TO DAM AND A HEAVY GROWTH OF TREES AND BUSHES TO EAT.

🐾 BEAVERS CAN GROW TO BE VERY BIG. SOME WEIGH AS MUCH AS 70 POUNDS.

🐾 A CLOSE RELATIVE OF THE BEAVER, THE MUSKRAT, MAY LIVE IN STREAMS OR MARSHES NEAR YOU!

BEAVER'S HIND FEET ARE WEBBED

A BEAVER SWIMMING USING TAIL AND WEBBED FEET

PEEK-A-BOO!

THE BEAVER'S WEBBED FEET SHOW IN TRACKS

ACTUAL SIZE ABOUT AS BIG AS YOUR FOOT

TAIL DRAGS

ACTUAL SIZE ABOUT AS BIG AS YOUR HAND

MUSKRATS DO NOT HAVE WEBBED FEET

BEAVER

MUSKRAT

13

Here are webbed footprints, but these aren't beaver
tracks. These tracks were made by an otter.

OTTER

OTTERS ARE IN THE WEASEL FAMILY. SO ARE MINKS, BADGERS, AND SKUNKS. (AND WEASELS!)

OTTERS CAN GROW TO BE 20 POUNDS OR MORE.

IF YOU LIVE NEAR A RIVER, YOU MAY HAVE AN OTTER LIVING NEAR YOU!

IF YOU LIVE NEAR A WOODLOT, LOOK FOR SOME OF OTTER'S WEASEL RELATIVES.

WEBBED HIND FEET

OTTER TRACKS SHOWING WEBBED FEET

ACTUAL SIZE IS 3 INCHES

TAIL DRAG

TRACKS OF AN OTTER RUNNING

OTTERS ARE THE ONLY WEASELS MORE AT HOME IN WATER THAN ON LAND.

Most of an otter's life is spent in a quiet underwater world.

An otter can outswim a trout! Can you see the otter catching the fish in this picture?

WHEEEE!

Otters are carefree critters. They play for hours, sliding down muddy spots on the pond bank and splashing into the water.

You may have seen otters sliding at the zoo.

These footprints look like the prints of tiny human hands and feet. They were made by raccoons.

Raccoons eat anything they can catch or find. They even raid garbage cans. They come to the water to hunt for crayfish, frogs, snails, and freshwater clams.

Like many wild animals, raccoons are nocturnal. That means they are more active at night than during the day.

RACCOON

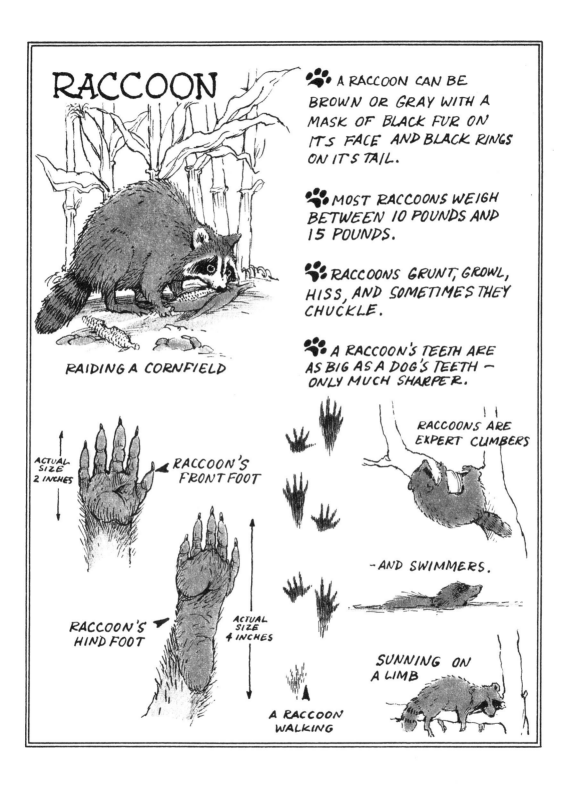

RAIDING A CORNFIELD

🐾 A RACCOON CAN BE BROWN OR GRAY WITH A MASK OF BLACK FUR ON ITS FACE AND BLACK RINGS ON ITS TAIL.

🐾 MOST RACCOONS WEIGH BETWEEN 10 POUNDS AND 15 POUNDS.

🐾 RACCOONS GRUNT, GROWL, HISS, AND SOMETIMES THEY CHUCKLE.

🐾 A RACCOON'S TEETH ARE AS BIG AS A DOG'S TEETH — ONLY MUCH SHARPER.

ACTUAL SIZE 2 INCHES

RACCOON'S FRONT FOOT

RACCOON'S HIND FOOT

ACTUAL SIZE 4 INCHES

A RACCOON WALKING

RACCOONS ARE EXPERT CLIMBERS

- AND SWIMMERS.

SUNNING ON A LIMB

One night I watched a raccoon reach under the rocks in the shallow water of the pond. It was feeling for a crayfish hiding there.

The raccoon looked like a bandit in the moonlight.

Here are lots of raccoon tracks in the mud. Follow them and see what they tell you. What did the big raccoons catch and eat? How many smaller raccoons were there?

A patch of woods is a good place to look for wildlife signs. Many of the shyest creatures live here. They hide among the trees and shadows. They eat twigs, buds, nuts, and seeds.

Deer tramp trails all through the woods as they search for food and water.

Look for the heart-shaped tracks of deer hooves in the mush of trampled leaves and soil.

WHITETAIL DEER

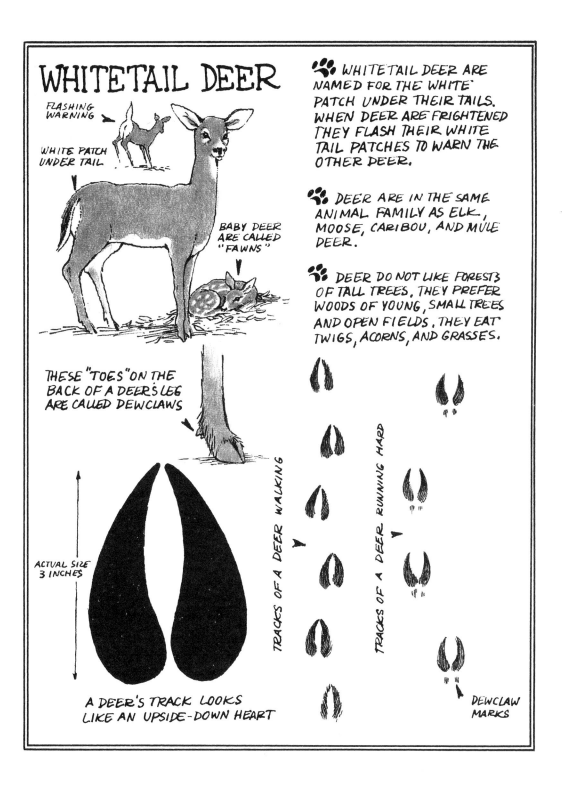

FLASHING WARNING →

WHITE PATCH UNDER TAIL →

BABY DEER ARE CALLED "FAWNS"

WHITETAIL DEER ARE NAMED FOR THE WHITE PATCH UNDER THEIR TAILS. WHEN DEER ARE FRIGHTENED THEY FLASH THEIR WHITE TAIL PATCHES TO WARN THE OTHER DEER.

DEER ARE IN THE SAME ANIMAL FAMILY AS ELK, MOOSE, CARIBOU, AND MULE DEER.

DEER DO NOT LIKE FORESTS OF TALL TREES. THEY PREFER WOODS OF YOUNG, SMALL TREES AND OPEN FIELDS. THEY EAT TWIGS, ACORNS, AND GRASSES.

THESE "TOES" ON THE BACK OF A DEER'S LEG ARE CALLED DEWCLAWS

ACTUAL SIZE 3 INCHES

A DEER'S TRACK LOOKS LIKE AN UPSIDE-DOWN HEART

TRACKS OF A DEER WALKING

TRACKS OF A DEER RUNNING HARD

DEWCLAW MARKS

Every summer the male deer, which are called bucks, grow antlers on their heads. During the time they are growing, antlers are covered with a layer of fuzzy skin called velvet. The velvet is filled with blood vessels that make the antlers grow quickly.

In autumn when a buck's antlers are fully grown, the velvet begins to dry up and peel. The bucks scrape it off by rubbing their antlers against the bark of small trees and bushes. This causes worn, smooth spots on the wood, which are called buck rubs.

Buck rubs are a sure sign that a buck has been using a trail.

Bucks fight with each other to see who will mate with the female deer, which are called does.

In winter after the mating season is over, antlers fall off. Each buck is left with two small smooth spots on his head, where antlers begin to grow again in spring.

Antlers that have fallen off are eaten by mice, squirrels, and other hungry forest nibblers. A buck has shed his antlers in this patch of winter woods. Can you find them?

Sometimes antlers fall off one at a time, so you might not find a set together.

Owls hunt at night. But I like to hunt for owls in the daytime. So can you. Here's how.

When an owl eats a mouse, it swallows it whole—tail and all.

◄ OWL PELLET
ACTUAL SIZE

The owl's stomach digests everything except the mouse bones and fur. The bones and fur form a ball that the owl coughs up and out onto the ground.

These balls of bones and fur are called owl pellets.
They collect on the ground around trees where owls
have been roosting. You can look for these pellets
around the trees near your home. If you find some,
look in the tree above for an owl sleeping the day away.
That's how I find owls in the daytime.

Here are some owl pellets. Can you see an owl in
this tree?

The beaver pond looks different in winter. It's frozen
and covered with snow.

When there's snow on the ground, it's easy to tell
which animals have been out and about.

Otters slide down snowy banks onto the slippery ice.
Deer tracks circle the pond where does and bucks have
eaten the tender tips of the snow-covered bushes.

The beavers are safe and warm in their lodge. They leave only to swim under the ice to their food supply, which they stored on the bottom of the pond during the fall.

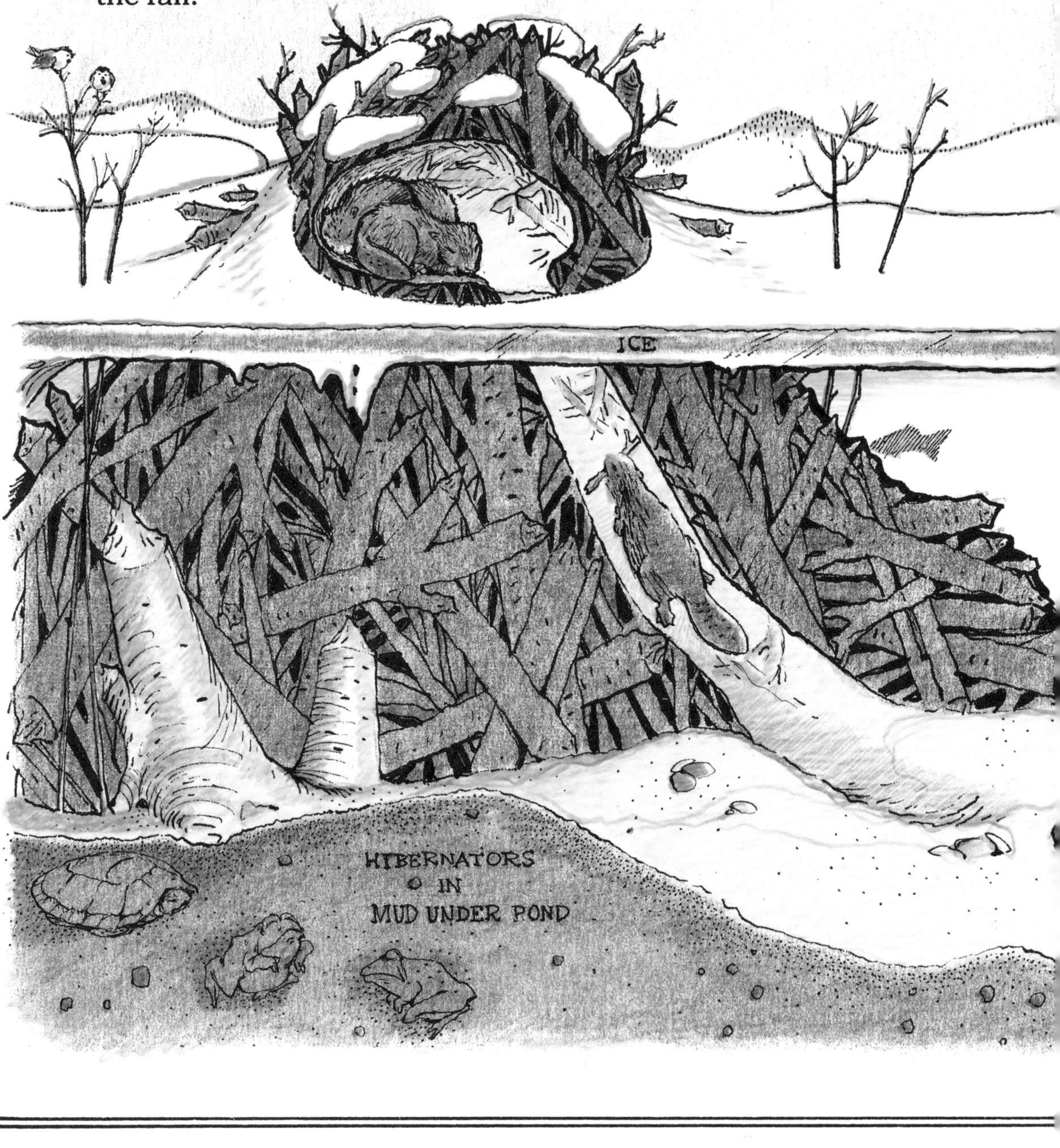

ICE

HIBERNATORS
IN
MUD UNDER POND

Snowshoe rabbits travel over the snow on the icy pond. Their huge hind feet leave broad tracks as they search for bark and twigs to eat.

When snow is soft and powdery, snowshoe rabbits stomp it down, making runways all through their feeding areas.

SNOWSHOE RABBIT

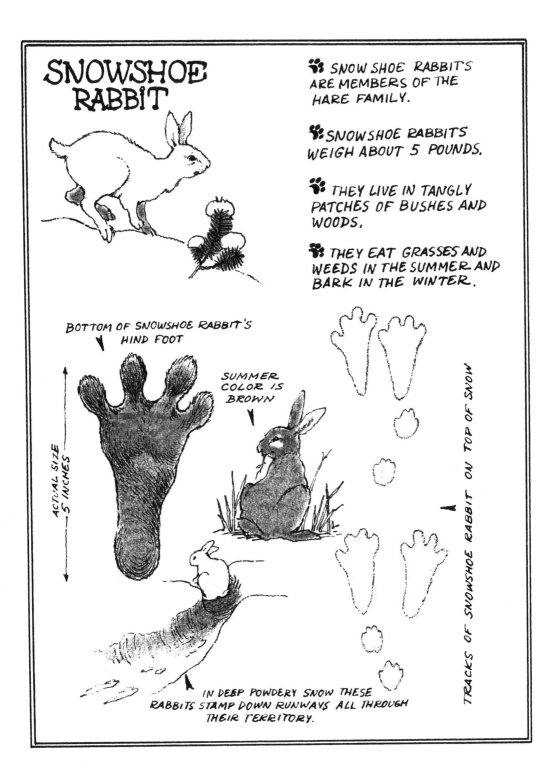

- SNOW SHOE RABBITS ARE MEMBERS OF THE HARE FAMILY.

- SNOWSHOE RABBITS WEIGH ABOUT 5 POUNDS.

- THEY LIVE IN TANGLY PATCHES OF BUSHES AND WOODS.

- THEY EAT GRASSES AND WEEDS IN THE SUMMER AND BARK IN THE WINTER.

BOTTOM OF SNOWSHOE RABBIT'S HIND FOOT

SUMMER COLOR IS BROWN

ACTUAL SIZE 5 INCHES

TRACKS OF SNOWSHOE RABBIT ON TOP OF SNOW

IN DEEP POWDERY SNOW THESE RABBITS STAMP DOWN RUNWAYS ALL THROUGH THEIR TERRITORY.

Snowshoe rabbits are sometimes called varying hares because their color varies, or changes, with the seasons. In summer they are brown and they blend in with the browns and greens of the forest. In winter their fur turns as white as snow, and you can hardly see them. They can hide from enemies by standing still in the snow.

Can you find six snowshoe rabbits in this picture?

These two sets of tracks belong to animals that hunt and eat rabbits. One set was made by a fox and one was made by a bobcat. Can you guess which is which without reading for a clue?

Bobcats live in dens in rocky areas. They have big hunting territories. Sometimes they travel far from home looking for food.

The bobcat is a wild relative of the house cat. All cats, including bobcats, can retract their claws. This means they can keep their claws folded back and away until they need them for climbing, fighting, or pouncing. Cats don't use their claws when they're walking or running, so claw marks rarely show in cat tracks.

Clawless pawprints are a sure sign that a cat has been around.

BOBCAT

BOBCATS ARE NAMED FOR THEIR SHORT, BOBBED TAILS.

BOBCATS CAN GROW TO BE TWICE THE SIZE OF A HOUSE CAT.

THEY ARE IN THE SAME ANIMAL FAMILY AS LIONS, TIGERS, COUGARS, AND HOUSE CATS.

BOBCATS WILL EAT SMALL ANIMALS, RABBITS, AND BIRDS.

RETRACTED CLAWS

SEE HOW THE CLAWS SHOW IN THE LUNGE.

ACTUAL SIZE ABOUT 2 INCHES

A BOBCAT DEN IN A ROCK PILE

TRACKS OF A WALKING CAT

TRACKS OF A CAT JUMPING AFTER A MOUSE

RUNWAY IN
RUNWAY OUT

Here are the tracks of those rabbit hunters again.
Now can you tell which are the fox's and which are the
bobcat's? You're right! The ones without claw marks are
the bobcat's.

Like the bobcat, the fox lives in a den that may be far
from where it makes its hunting rounds.

The fox and the dog belong to the same family—the
canine family. A dog's footprints and a fox's footprints
look very much alike. But when a fox walks, it places
one foot directly in front of the other, leaving a trail
much narrower than a dog's.

RED FOX

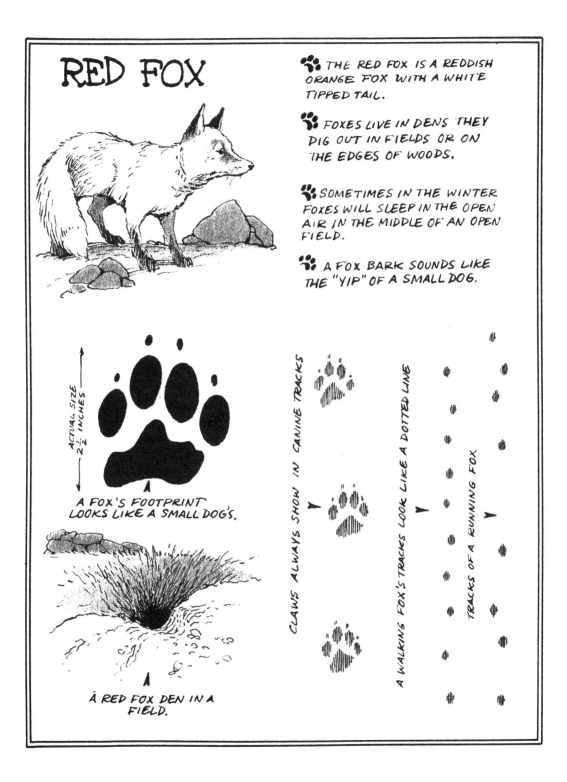

🐾 THE RED FOX IS A REDDISH ORANGE FOX WITH A WHITE TIPPED TAIL.

🐾 FOXES LIVE IN DENS THEY DIG OUT IN FIELDS OR ON THE EDGES OF WOODS.

🐾 SOMETIMES IN THE WINTER FOXES WILL SLEEP IN THE OPEN AIR IN THE MIDDLE OF AN OPEN FIELD.

🐾 A FOX BARK SOUNDS LIKE THE "YIP" OF A SMALL DOG.

ACTUAL SIZE 2½ INCHES

A FOX'S FOOTPRINT LOOKS LIKE A SMALL DOG'S.

A RED FOX DEN IN A FIELD.

CLAWS ALWAYS SHOW IN CANINE TRACKS

A WALKING FOX'S TRACKS LOOK LIKE A DOTTED LINE

TRACKS OF A RUNNING FOX

Follow these tracks on the snow-covered pond. Can you follow the fox? Where did the bobcat go? A rabbit-hunting beagle has also been on the pond. Don't get them confused!

A hungry fox prowling around a pond would stop to inspect these tracks. They were made by a grouse.

The brushy area around the beaver pond is a good place for grouse to live. In summer they can find plenty of leaves and insects to eat. In winter they can travel easily over the snow, eating twigs and winter buds.

Grouse walk as often as they fly.

Tracks in the snow are good grouse signs to look for.

Sometimes in winter grouse fly and dive, or plunge, into soft snow, making holes big enough to stay in. They keep warm underneath the snow, away from the cold air. A plunge hole in the snow is another good grouse sign to look for.

During the Blizzard of '77, I dove headfirst into a snowbank, thinking I'd spend the night in there, safe and warm. But the snowbank turned out to be a snow-covered boulder, and I went home with a lump on my noggin!

Once in a while, grouse make the same mistake.

BLUE JAY

WING PRINTS

Some birds walk and some birds hop. For instance, a crow is a walker. Blue jays and sparrows are hoppers.

Can you guess which bird has made each set of tracks? My animal-track chart on pages 44–45 will help you.

CROW

SPARROW

BIG DOG

SMALL DOG OR FOX

CHIPMUNK

SKUNK

WEASEL

HOUSE CAT

RACCOON

MUSKRAT

COTTONTAIL
RABBIT

MOUSE

RAT

44

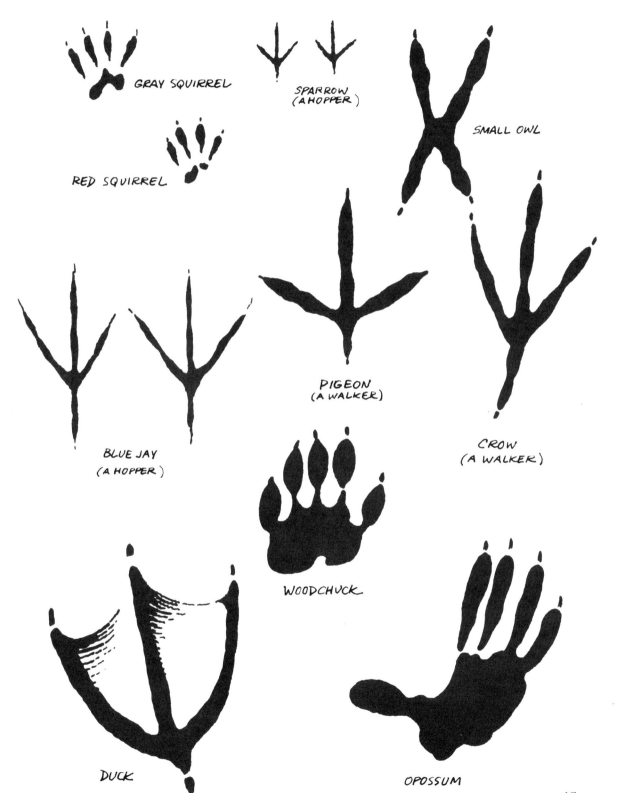

GRAY SQUIRREL

SPARROW
(A HOPPER)

SMALL OWL

RED SQUIRREL

PIGEON
(A WALKER)

CROW
(A WALKER)

BLUE JAY
(A HOPPER)

WOODCHUCK

DUCK

OPOSSUM

45

I've seen a lot of tracks here in the forest. I've even tracked fleas through the fur on a bear's back. But I can't seem to recognize these tracks next to my own.

Why, they must be yours.

Wherever you live, there are animals living near you. Look for the signs animals leave in parks and woodlots, on pavements and sidewalks, under trees, around streams and ponds, and in the snow. I can't promise you'll find any flea tracks, but you'll find something. And if you hear a soft swish in the night, go back to sleep. It's just a fox turning around somewhere in the forest.

INDEX